My Name Is Not Dummy

Written by Elizabeth Crary   Illustrated by Marina Megale

Parenting Press, Inc.

SEATTLE, WASHINGTON

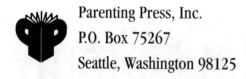

Parenting Press, Inc.
P.O. Box 75267
Seattle, Washington 98125

Ways to teach children how to solve social problems are thoroughly explained in Problem-Solving Techniques in Childrearing *by Myrna B. Shure and George Spivack, San Francisco: Jossey-Bass Publishers, 1978.*

Book design by Elizabeth Watson
Formatting by Margarite D. Hargrave

Library of Congress Cataloging-in-Publication Data
Crary, Elizabeth, 1942-
      My name is not dummy / by Elizabeth Crary ; illustrated by Marina Megale. -- 2nd ed.
        p. cm. -- (A children's problem solving book)
      Summary: Using a story about two friends, Jenny and Eduardo, explores the various ways Jenny might react when Eduardo calls her a dummy, and the consequences of her possible reactions.
      ISBN 1-884734-17-0 (lib. bdg.). -- ISBN 1-884734-16-2 (paper)
      1. Problem solving--Juvenile literature.   2. Conflict (Psychology)--Juvenile literature.
[1. Problem solving.   2. Conflict (Psychology)   3. Interpersonal relations.]   I. Megale, Marina, ill.   II. Title.   III. Series: Crary, Elizabeth, 1942-   Children's problem solving book.
BF441.C73   1996
158'.25--dc20

                                           96-20259
                                            CIP

Parents (and Others) Can Teach Children How to Think

I wrote the six *Children's Problem Solving Books* to help children learn
to solve social problems. Each book explores a common problem for children:
sharing, waiting, wanting, being lost, and name calling. These books are interactive,
and children have fun thinking about the questions. Your young listener/reader will
enjoy helping the children in the stories decide what to do to solve their problems.

Why These Books Look Different

These books look different because they do
something different. They teach children to think
about the problems they face. These books help in
three ways. First, they model a process for thinking
before acting. Second, they offer children several
different ways to handle each situation. Third, they
show children how one person's behavior affects
other people. Research shows that the more ideas a
child has to solve social problems, the better his or
her social adjustment is.

How to Use These Books

You will find questions to ask your child on almost
every page. Before you read the *italic* words, give
your child time to think about the question and
answer it her- or himself. Each time a CHOICE (in the
gray box) is offered, let her or him choose what to
do. Turn to the page selected to see what happens.
There are no "right" or "wrong" answers. All
alternatives teach children to think. The outcomes
of each allow children to discover for themselves
why some actions are more effective than others.

I have included questions about feelings to
encourage children to think about how they and
others feel when there is a problem. Children need
to know that feelings are not "good" or "bad," they
just are. Awareness of feelings helps children think
of solutions that meet their own and other's needs.

Transition from Story to Real Life

The last page of each book invites readers to list
their own ideas about other ways to solve the story
child's problem. With guidance your child can use
the techniques learned in the book to think of ways
to solve problems he or she has. For children who
are reluctant to talk about solutions to their
personal problems, you can ask them what the
character in the book might do in a situation similar
to theirs.

Through reading these books you are helping
your child learn how to make good decisions.
Further, you are teaching her or him that thinking
and learning are fun. Children learn to think by
thinking, not by being told what to do. Give your
child many opportunities to practice thinking and
problem solving. Have fun!

Elizabeth Crary
Seattle, Washington

This is a story about Jenny and Eduardo.
Usually they have lots of fun together.
They play and talk and sing.

But sometimes they have troubles. Like now!
Jenny was playing with Eduardo.
Then Eduardo called her a dummy.
Jenny doesn't like to be called a dummy.

What can Jenny do so Eduardo won't call her a dummy?
(Wait for child to respond after each question. Look at page 3, "How to Use These Books," for ways to encourage children to think for themselves.)

CHOICES
Jenny can think of nine ideas. She can—

What will she try first?
(Wait for child to respond. Then turn to the appropriate page and continue the story.)

6

Cry

Jenny decides to cry.

She says, "I'm not a dummy."

Eduardo says, "Yes, you are."

Jenny cries harder.

Eduardo then begins to chant, "You are a cry baby! You are a cry baby!"

How does Jenny feel?

Sad and mad. Sad because she doesn't know what to do. Mad because she doesn't like to be called a dummy or cry baby.

CHOICES

What do you think Jenny will do next?

Call Eduardo a dummy . . . . *page 10*

Tell on Eduardo . . . . *page 12*

Call Eduardo a dummy

Jenny decides to call Eduardo a dummy.

Jenny goes up to Eduardo and says, "You are a dummy, too."

Eduardo says, "No, you're a dummy."

Jenny says, "No, I'm not."

Eduardo says, "Yes, you are."

How does Jenny feel now?

Mad. Mad that Eduardo still called her a dummy.

How does Eduardo feel?

Mad, too. Mad that Jenny called him a dummy.

CHOICES

What will Jenny do now?

Tell on Eduardo . . . . *page 12*

Ignore unkind words . . . . *page 16*

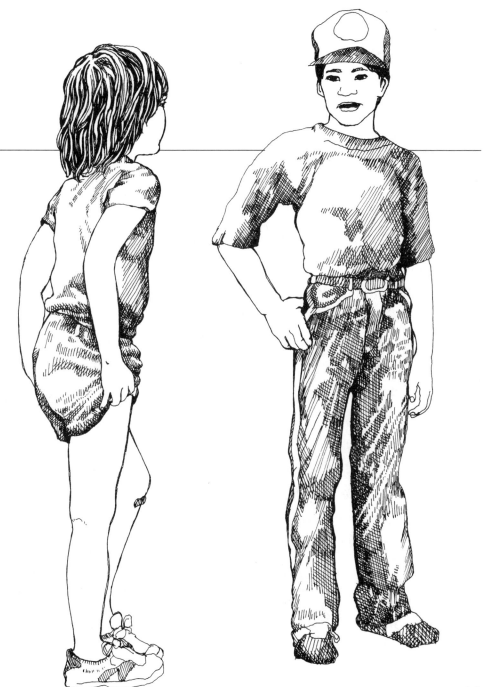

Tell on Eduardo

Jenny decides to tell a grown-up. "Marie, Eduardo called me a dummy. He is mean."

Marie asks, "Jenny, are you a dummy?"

"No," Jenny answers.

"Well, Jenny, you can decide if you want to be upset or not. Do you want to be upset?" asks Marie.

"No," Jenny answers.

"Okay. Then you can find something to do instead. If you need some ideas, come and ask me."

How does Jenny feel?

Sad and happy. Sad that Eduardo called her a dummy. Happy because she doesn't have to believe him.

CHOICES
What will Jenny do now?
   Tell Eduardo how she feels. . . . . *page 14*
   Ask for help . . . . *page 18*

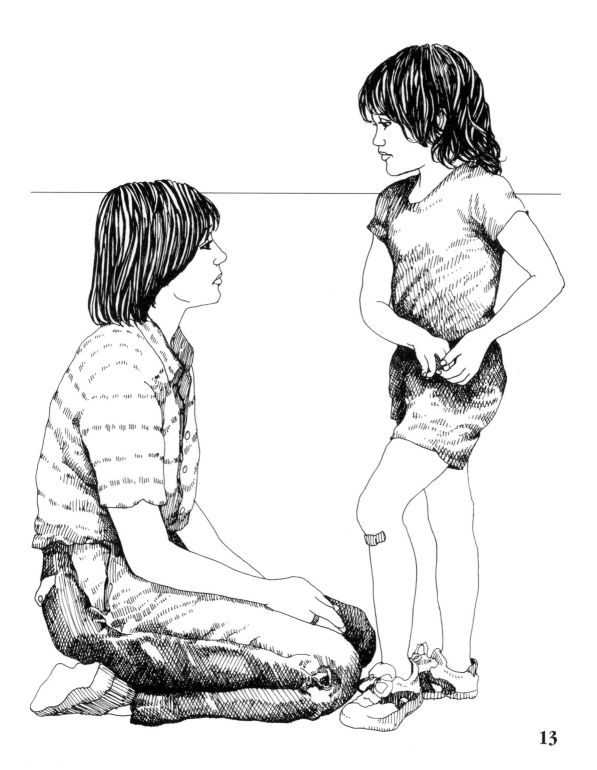

Tell Eduardo how she feels

Jenny decides to tell Eduardo how she feels.

Jenny says, "When you call me a dummy, I feel hurt and mad."

"You are a dummy," Eduardo replies.

"Calling me a dummy doesn't make me one," Jenny answers.

Eduardo replies, "I don't care. I am mad, too."

How does Jenny feel?

Happy and mad. Happy that she told Eduardo how she feels. Mad because Eduardo said he didn't care.

CHOICES

What will Jenny do now?

Find someone else to play with . . . . *page 24*

Ask Eduardo why he called her a dummy . . . . *page 26*

14

Ignore unkind words

Jenny decides to ignore the name calling.

She begins to brush her dog. Eduardo calls her a dummy. She pretends not to hear him.

He begins to chant, "Jenny is a dummy! Jenny is a dummy!"

Jenny thinks of two reasons why she isn't a dummy. She thinks she has good ideas, and she brushes her dog well.

After a while Eduardo quits and goes away.

How does Jenny feel?

Sad and glad. Sad that Eduardo left without playing with her. Glad because she knows she is not a dummy.

How do you like this ending?

What could Jenny do if Eduardo continued to call her a dummy?

(Turn to page 18.)

Ask for help

Jenny decides to ask Marie for help.

"Marie, I feel bad when Eduardo calls me a dummy. What can I do?" Jenny asks.

Marie answers, "I know three things you can do.

"You can make up a good word in your mind, and pretend Eduardo is calling you that.

"You can think of smart things you do, and remember them when he calls you a dummy.

"You can do something really unexpected."

"If you need more ideas let me know."

How does Jenny feel?

Happy. She has several ideas she can use if Eduardo calls her a dummy.

(Turn to page 20.)

"Marie, what would be unexpected?" Jenny asks.

"Saying something silly, like 'thank you' or 'Yes, it is a beautiful day,'" Marie replied.

"Why would that do any good?" Jenny wondered aloud.

"Well," Marie answered, "usually when someone calls you a dummy, they are angry with something you or someone else did. They often want to make you mad or sad. You don't have to be mad or sad just because someone wants you to. You can decide if you want to get mad or sad, or not."

CHOICES
What will Jenny do now?

    Do something unexpected . . . . *page 22*

    Find someone else to play with . . . . *page 24*

Do something unexpected

Jenny decides to try doing something unexpected.

Eduardo repeats, "Jenny is a dummy."

Jenny says, "Thank you."

Eduardo asks, "Why did you say 'Thank you'?"

Jenny answers, "Because it is better than being bored."

Eduardo does not say anything.

"Would you like to play something?" Jenny asks.

"I guess so," Eduardo says.

How does Jenny feel?

Good. She and Eduardo are going to play together.

How does Eduardo feel?

Surprised. He tried to make Jenny mad, but she did not get mad.

How do you like this ending?

Find someone else to play with

Jenny decides she will find someone else to play with.
She sees Anna, who is playing softball.
"Anna, may I play ball with you?" she asks.
"Oh, yes. That will be fun. We need more kids on our team," replies Anna.

How does Jenny feel?
   Sad and glad. Sad that Eduardo is mad at her. Glad because she has Anna to play with.

How do you like this ending?

   (Turn the page to see what else Jenny could do.)

Ask Eduardo why he called her a dummy

Jenny decides to ask Eduardo why he called her a dummy.

"Eduardo, why did you call me a dummy?"

"Because you wouldn't play spaceship," Eduardo answers.

"I don't want to just sit in a spaceship. That's boring," Jenny replies.

(Turn to page 28.)

27

"What do you want to do instead?" Eduardo asks.

"I don't know. What do you want to do?" Jenny responds.

"We could play tag. Okay?" asks Eduardo.

"Yeah," Jenny replies, "that's a good idea!"

How does Jenny feel?

Happy. Happy because Eduardo has stopped calling her a dummy. Happy because she and Eduardo can play together.

How does Eduardo feel?

Happy, too. Happy because he and Jenny can play something they both want to play.

Do you like this ending?

Idea page

Here is a list of Jenny's ideas.
Start your own list of things you can do when someone calls you a dummy.
   Add more ideas as you think of them.

Jenny's ideas	Your ideas
✓ Cry	✎
✓ Call Eduardo a dummy	✎
✓ Tell on Eduardo	
✓ Tell Eduardo how she feels	✎
✓ Ignore unkind words	✎
✓ Think of reasons she's not a dummy	✎
✓ Ask for help	✎
✓ Do something unexpected	
✓ Find someone else to play with	✎
✓ Ask Eduardo why he called her a dummy	✎
✓ Ask Eduardo what he wants to play	✎
	✎

30

Solving social problems ...

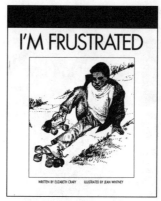

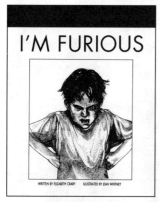